Thanksgiving Jokes
Funny Jokes for Kids

Arnie Lightning

Arnie Lightning Books

ISBN-13: 978-1535379939
ISBN-10: 1535379936

"*A day without laughter is a day wasted.*"

–Charlie Chaplin

CONTENTS

FREE GIFT

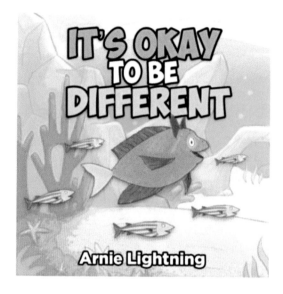

"It's Okay to Be Different" is a beautifully illustrated story about accepting and celebrating others for their differences. It's a great way to teach children to appreciate and accept others for who they are.

To claim your FREE GIFT, simply go to www.ArnieLightning.com/freegift and enter your email address. Shortly thereafter, I will send you a free eBook for you to enjoy!

Please visit: www.ArnieLightning.com/freegift

FUNNY THANKSGIVING JOKES

Q: What is the best thing to put in a pumpkin pie?

A: Your teeth!

Q: What is a pumpkin's favorite game?

A: Squash!

Q: What kind of key cannot unlock a door?

A: A tur<u>key</u>!

Q: What part of a turkey has the most feathers?

A: The outside!

Q: How does Thanksgiving always end?

A: With the letter G!

Q: What is purple and blue and has a lot of feathers?

A: A turkey holding its breath for too long!

Q: How do you know the Indians were the first people in North America?

A: Because they had reservations!

Q: What did the monster say to the Thanksgiving turkey?

A: I am pleased to eat you!

Q: Why did the Pilgrims first eat turkey on Thanksgiving?

A: Because they could not fit a moose in the oven!

Q: Why was Thanksgiving invented?

A: Another excuse to watch football!

Q: What did the army general do on Thanksgiving?

A: He gave tanks!

Q: What is black and white and red all over?

A: A pilgrim with poison ivy!

Q: What bird has wings but cannot fly?

A: A roasted turkey!

Q: Why was the turkey thrown in jail?

A: He was suspected of fowl play!

Q: Did you hear about the crazy turkey?

A: He was ready for Thanksgiving!

Q: Why was the Thanksgiving soup so expensive?

A: It was made of 24 carrots!

Q: What is brown and white and flies all over?

A: A Thanksgiving turkey being carved with a chain saw!

Q: What do you get when you cross a Thanksgiving dessert and a monster?

A: Bumpkin pie!

Q: What is a turkey's favorite dessert?

A: Peach gobbler!

Q: Can you spell Indian house with only two letters?

A: TP!

Q: Who is never hungry on Thanksgiving?

A: A turkey because it is always stuffed!

Q: Why did the pilgrim's pants keep falling down?

A: Because they wore belt buckles on their hat!

Q: How come the large man did not get a second helping of pecan pie?

A: Because he ate it all the first time!

Q: What was the Pilgrim's favorite dance?

A: The Plymouth Rock!

Q: What do vampires put on their mashed potatoes?

A: Grave-y!

Q: Which country never celebrates Thanksgiving?

A: Turkey!

Q: Why did the turkey cross the road?

A: Because he wanted to prove that he wasn't chicken!

Q: What did the turkey say to the turkey hunter?

A: Quack! Quack! Quack! Quack!

Q: Where did the pilgrims land when they came to America?

A: They landed on their feet!

Q: What do you get when you cross a turkey and an octopus?

A: Enough drumsticks to feed the entire family!

Q: What did the snowman eat for Thanksgiving?

A: An ice-burger!

Q: How do you stuff a turkey?

A: Buy him two large pizzas and some cheeseburgers!

Q: Why did the monster get a ticket on Thanksgiving?

A: Because he exceeded the feed limit!

Q: What smells so good at Thanksgiving?

A: Your nose!

Q: Why did the turkey hunter shoot the turkey?

A: He was in a fowl mood!

MAZE #1

MAZE #2

MAZE #3

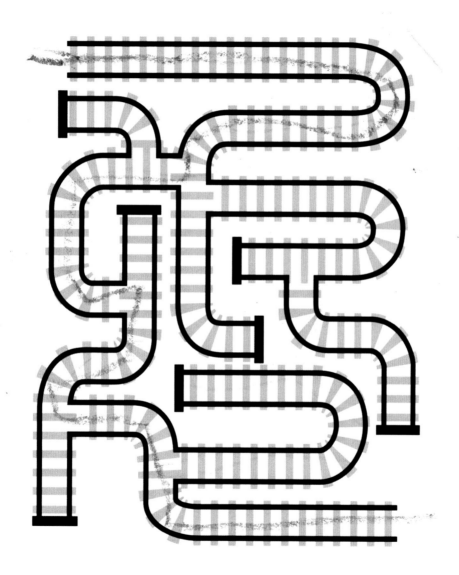

MAZE #4

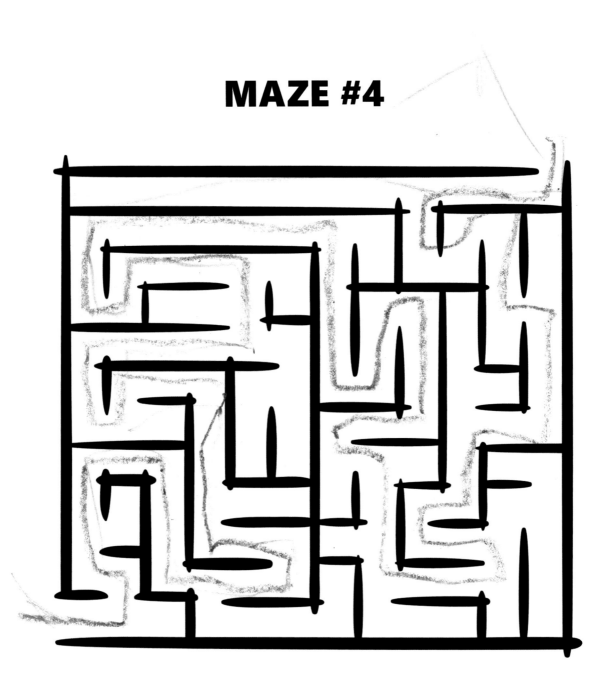

SOLUTIONS

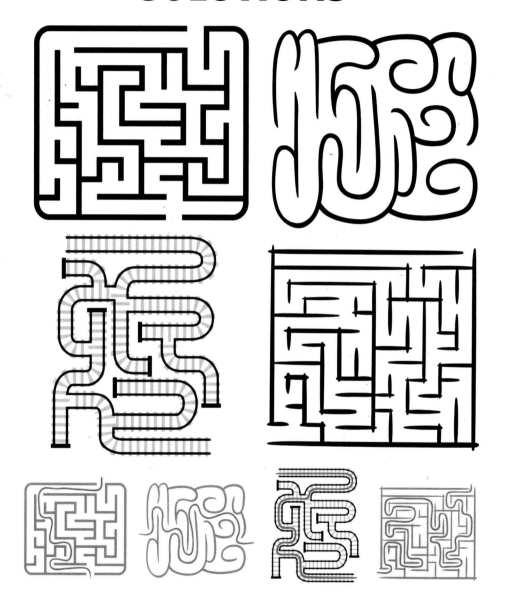

ABOUT THE AUTHOR

Arnie Lightning is a dreamer. He believes that everyone should dream big and not be afraid to take chances to make their dreams come true. Arnie enjoys writing, reading, doodling, and traveling. In his free time, he likes to play video games and run. Arnie lives in Mississippi where he graduated from The University of Southern Mississippi in Hattiesburg, MS.

For more books by Arnie Lightning please visit:
www.ArnieLightning.com/books

Q why did the turkey go to thanksgivin dinner?

A because he was featherd u

Made in the USA
Middletown, DE
17 November 2019